Snowed In with Grandmother Silk

by CAROL FENNER
Illustrated by AMANDA HARVEY

PUFFIN BOOKS

PUFFIN BOOKS
Published by the Penguin Group
Penguin Young Readers Group, 345 Hudson Street, New York, New York 10014, U.S.A.
Penguin Group (Canada), 10 Alcorn Avenue, Toronto, Ontario, Canada M4V 3B2
(a division of Pearson Penguin Canada Inc.)
Penguin Books Ltd, 80 Strand, London WC2R 0RL, England
Penguin Ireland, 25 St Stephen's Green, Dublin 2, Ireland
(a division of Penguin Books Ltd)
Penguin Group (Australia), 250 Camberwell Road, Camberwell, Victoria 3124, Australia
(a division of Pearson Australia Group Pty Ltd)
Penguin Books India Pvt Ltd, 11 Community Centre, Panchsheel Park,
New Delhi - 110 017, India
Penguin Group (NZ), Cnr Airborne and Rosedale Roads, Albany, Auckland 1310, New Zealand
(a division of Pearson New Zealand Ltd)
Penguin Books (South Africa) (Pty) Ltd, 24 Sturdee Avenue, Rosebank,
Johannesburg 2196, South Africa

Registered Offices: Penguin Books Ltd, 80 Strand, London WC2R 0RL, England

First published in the United States of America by Dial Books for Young Readers,
a division of Penguin Young Readers Group, 2003
Published by Puffin Books, a division of Penguin Young Readers Group, 2005

Designed by Jasmin Rubero
Text set in Adobe Caslon

5 7 9 10 8 6

THE LIBRARY OF CONGRESS HAS CATALOGED THE DIAL EDITION AS FOLLOWS:
Fenner, Carol.
Snowed in with Grandmother Silk / by Carol Fenner ; illustrations by Amanda Harvey.
p.   cm.
Summary: Ruddy is disappointed when his parents go on a cruise and he must stay
with his fussy grandmother for ten days, but an unexpected snowstorm reveals
a surprising side of Grandmother Silk.
[1. Grandmothers—Fiction. 2. Snow—Fiction.]
I. Harvey, Amanda, ill. II. Title.
PZ7.F342 Sn 2003 [Fic]—dc21 2002152296
ISBN 0-8037-2857-3

Puffin ISBN 978-0-14-240472-0
Manufactured in China

Jiles Williams, Carol Fenner's husband,
wishes to extend his warmest thanks
to the following people for their
generous help and enthusiasm:

*Betty Horvath, Ardyce Czuchna-Curl,
Wendy Risk, Bonnie Alkema,
Maris Soule, and Susan Rowe*

To Christopher

A.H.

Chapter One

Ruddy didn't much like going to Silver Lake, even in summertime. Grandmother Silk wasn't fun to visit. She called him Rudford, not Ruddy. She was not like Granny Nancy, who told him stories and could find cool sites on her computer—

dragon stuff and sword-fighting, trucks and how they work inside.

Grandmother Silk didn't play computer games or any other games. She didn't take walks. She didn't like loud voices, even if you were only scaring the Canada geese by the water to study how they took off across Silver Lake.

Grandmother Silk didn't like running, even if you were running from a great big goose flapping his terrible wings at you.

She wore high heels all the time. Even her bedroom slippers had high heels. Her hair was piled into neat, unmoving curls that Ruddy's mother called "designer hair."

Grandmother Silk was his father's mother. She lived in a big old house with a lot of rooms inside, and a lot of trees outside. The TV at Grandmother Silk's was hidden in a big cabinet that matched the furniture. His grandmother only watched *Masterpiece Theatre* on Tuesday nights at nine. The rest of the time, the doors on the TV cabinet stayed closed. Ruddy always brought along an armload of books for summer visits.

Behind the big old house was a garden for tomatoes and herbs and other stuff. Only Lucy, who came to cook every day, was allowed to pick anything from the vegetable garden, even if Ruddy felt hungry for a sweet, little, warm red tomato.

In front of the house was a beautiful garden of roses and lilies and other stuff. No one was allowed to pick a flower from this garden, even if Ruddy only wanted to surprise a smile from Grandmother Silk with a perfect pink lily and didn't mean to pull up the whole bulb.

Joe Penny came every day, too, to work in Grandmother Silk's gardens. He mowed the lawns and mended things that were broken.

"What do you do in winter?" Ruddy asked.

"I shovel snow," said Joe Penny. "I chop wood. I lay fires in the fireplaces."

"For Grandmother Silk to light when she's cold?" asked Ruddy.

"Oh, the electric furnace down in the basement warms the house," said Joe Penny. "The wood fires are to stare at."

Sometimes Joe Penny let Ruddy help with the weeding, even though Grandmother Silk didn't like him to get dirty.

When Lucy came to cook, she picked herbs and vegetables from the garden. Then she fixed delicious food. She put thyme and peas with chicken and gravy and baked them under a buttery crust. She made biscuits for breakfast with a tomato parsley omelet. Lucy let Ruddy help mix up cake or pudding, even though Grandmother Silk didn't like him to get sticky.

He must, as his mother often said, think of the good things.

One good thing about Silver Lake besides Joe Penny and Lucy's food was plenty of time to read. Also, Grandmother

Silk always took Ruddy to the zoo. She said it was educational.

"Zoos are worthwhile visits," she told Ruddy, "because of the education you take in while you think you're only having fun. Besides, the creatures live inside heavy glass and cages. We are safe, even from snakes." She gave a small shudder.

Joe Penny always drove them to the zoo and waited in front of the gates in the big black car. Grandmother Silk didn't last long walking around in her high heels. She had to sit down a lot. She let Ruddy visit the lions and giraffes and monkeys as long as she could always see where he was. She held a little handkerchief over her nose most of the time.

"Don't step in anything," she warned. But Ruddy liked the zoo smell. Their zoo visits were never long enough for him to get all the education he wanted.

Chapter Two

Ruddy had never been to Silver Lake in autumn. He had never seen Joe Penny chop wood or lay a fire. He had never seen the trees on Grandmother Silk's lawn turn yellow and red. He had never seen a zillion Canada geese fly over the lake, nor heard their honk-honk-honk grow faint as they traveled south.

And he didn't want to, either.

But one autumn his mother and father decided to take a cruise. They would be gone right through Halloween. His other grandma was away visiting Ruddy's new baby cousin in Texas, so he couldn't stay with her.

Ruddy knew, in one heavy moment, that he was going to Grandmother Silk's for ten whole days. He wouldn't get to trick-or-treat on his street. He would miss his school Halloween party. Ruddy started his attack immediately, weak as it was.

"I probably won't even get a costume," he complained to his mother.

"How about last year's? No one at Silver Lake has seen it."

"I'm bigger now. I'm eight. Too old for a Snoopy suit. My feet would poke through the bottom."

His mother smiled. "That's true. Or you'd have to bend over to walk."

She laughed. "I'm sorry, Ruddy. I have this sad picture of a bent-over Snoopy." His mother kept on laughing.

It was hard to keep feeling rotten when his mother laughed like that.

But Ruddy didn't want to laugh. And he didn't want to go to Grandmother Silk's.

He found his father sitting on an up-turned pail by the garden. He was weeding.

"It's a terrible time for a cruise," Ruddy said to his father.

"Should we do it at Christmas, then?" asked his father.

"No!" cried Ruddy. "That's worse."

"Your teacher is giving you some lessons to do at your grandmother's," said his father. "So you won't get behind."

Well, homework will give me something to do, thought Ruddy. He hoped there would be some stuff about prehistoric animals and birds. And he liked math, making numbers come out right. Maybe Joe Penny will let me help chop wood, he thought. Maybe he will show me about laying a fire. He thought of Lucy's biscuits, and that was a good thing, too.

"It's a terrible time for a cruise, Rudford," said Grandmother Silk on the first day of his visit. Well, she isn't so dumb, thought Ruddy.

"We'll go to the zoo for Halloween," she said. "They have a party of some sort there. As what animal do you wish to disguise yourself?"

"A black panther!" Ruddy shouted. His grandmother winced. Had he been too loud?

"No," said Ruddy in a careful, quiet voice. "Make that a gorilla."

Though ferocious, a black panther was too quiet an animal. A gorilla could beat his chest and roar.

"We'll go early and get a costume at the zoo shop," said his grandmother.

Things are looking up, thought Ruddy. Grandmother Silk would sit on a bench in her high heels while Ruddy took a quick spin around the zoo. He wanted to check out the real gorilla more carefully, see how a gorilla sat or stood leaning into one long arm.

Joe Penny came, and Ruddy watched him lay a fire. Joe Penny explained. "You see here, you have to crumple paper and stack the kindling on top so there's air between. Fire needs to breathe."

Ruddy watched him arrange the kindling like a nest.

"Then you have to settle the logs so they

don't smother the kindling. Air is as important as dry wood to a fire." He wrinkled a smile at Ruddy.

"Before I leave," said Ruddy, "maybe I can try it?" When Joe Penny nodded, Ruddy thought again that things were looking up. He would lay a fire. He would visit the zoo as a gorilla and go to a party. The time would pass quickly until he could go home again.

Several evenings later, his mother and father called from the cruise ship.

"How are you doing?" his mother asked.

"Fine. How's the cruise?"

"It's just beautiful here, Ruddy," his mother gushed. "The water is so dark and still. The breezes are warm and the moon is as bright as a golden doubloon." She sighed. "And how are you faring with Grandmother Silk?"

"I'm going to a Halloween party at the zoo," Ruddy was happy to tell his mother. "What's a doubloon?"

"Some kind of ancient golden coin. The moon looks absolutely—"

"This is costing us a fortune, Eve," Ruddy heard his father grump in the background.

"Don't you want to talk to your son?" his mother teased. His father must have grabbed the phone, because he heard a little squeal from his mom.

"Rud. How's things? Take it easy on

your grandmother. Have fun if you can. We'll be home before too long. See you later, pal."

Ruddy heard a funny hollow click as his father disconnected the phone.

"Bye, Dad," he said.

He tried very hard to think good thoughts. Luckily, Halloween was only a day away.

Chapter Three

Lucy came and brought short ribs to fix for dinner. She cooked them for a long time, until they were gravy-brown and falling off the bone.

"Lucy knows how to get all the fat rendered out of short ribs," said Grandmother

Silk proudly, as if she'd done the ribs herself.

Later Lucy took green beans from the freezer. She had picked them from the garden last summer.

"Sweet potatoes, mashed, or noodles?" she asked Ruddy.

"I'm worried," said Ruddy. "I'm worried that the gorilla suit may be gone from the zoo. Someone else might see what a perfect costume it is. Halloween is in one day."

"Sweet potatoes, mashed, or noodles?"

"Noodles," said Ruddy a little sullenly.

Then Lucy said, "I'll run and ask your grandmother if Joe Penny can take you over now while dinner is fixing. You can get your costume and then you can practice being a gorilla."

Ruddy crossed his fingers. Lucy could often work magic with Grandmother Silk.

When Lucy returned she said, "You can go, but no noise. Your grandmother says you must practice silently."

Ruddy was elated. He could practice chest-beating quietly, and standing and walking and gorilla-sitting.

They went right away—Joe Penny and Ruddy in the long black car, quickly, so they wouldn't be late for dinner. Grandmother Silk gave Joe Penny a bunch of money.

The zoo was closing, but Zooboutique

was still open. Ruddy could see a few customers inside. He hurried through the Halloween-decorated door and rushed to the racks of costumes. There he was, Mr. Gorilla. Not in the racks but displayed on a stand in the center of the room. A freckle-faced girl was trailing her hand lovingly down his hairy arms. Ruddy raced to the salesclerk, shouting, "That gorilla suit, please! I brought money for Mr. Gorilla!"

"We have one in the racks, young man." The salesclerk smiled. She pulled out another gorilla suit. It wasn't nearly as hairy. Its face wasn't nearly as fierce nor its arms as long.

"Not him," cried Ruddy. *"Him!"* He ran to Mr. Gorilla.

"Lucky!" said the freckle-faced girl as the clerk took the hairy suit from the display and held it up.

"Lucky," the freckle-faced girl repeated as Mr. Gorilla was wrapped up. "I'm wearing last year's fairy tutu. It's too small and I'm too old."

Ruddy turned to the girl. "It won't matter once the fun starts," he said politely. But he wondered if this were really true. He wouldn't have wanted to be a bent-over Snoopy.

"It will get really hot under that suit," said the girl. Her voice was wistful, as if being too hot in a gorilla suit was something to be longed for.

Ruddy waved to her as Joe Penny drove them home in the long black car. They were just in time for dinner.

Chapter Four

That night, the night before Halloween, there was a terrible surprise. A snowstorm came howling through. Ruddy and Grandmother Silk sat in front of the fireplace, staring at the fire. Outside they could hear branches with frozen leaves slap at the house. Suddenly, the lights went out, and

Grandmother Silk had to search around in the dark of the garage for a flashlight to light their way to bed.

Early in the morning, a huge tree came crashing down right in front of Grandmother Silk's big old house.

Outside the window of his room, past the leaves of the fallen tree, the sky was gray. Snow fell in clumps from the other trees. Ruddy got up. The light in the bathroom wouldn't go on, so he decided to hold it. He crawled back into bed. He wished for his dog, Buster, who slept on his bed at home. He wished for his mom and dad. They would let him crawl into their bed. His dad would grumble at Ruddy's cold toes, but they would all snuggle down under the covers, cozy warm, with Buster lying at their feet.

"Don't wet the bed," his father might say. Of course not, thought Ruddy. His father sometimes sounded like Grandmother Silk.

Ruddy began to get hungry. He thought of bacon and Lucy's biscuits. He thought of strawberry jam. He got hungrier. He thought of Lucy's pancakes with butter and maple syrup. No one called him to breakfast. He got hungrier and hungrier, and now he really had to go to the bathroom. It was too cold to get out of bed.

Finally Grandmother Silk came into his room. She was wearing her high heels and a dark mink coat over a black suit and white sweater. She walked to his window and looked out at the big fallen tree.

"Why are we having snow in October?" she asked Ruddy's window.

"Yeah," said Ruddy. "It's Halloween."

"Someone will come," said Grandmother Silk. "You'd better get up and dressed."

Ruddy looked around his cold, cold room. Then he unwrapped Mr. Gorilla's rough, furry body. The freckle-faced girl had said, "It will get really hot under that suit." I hope so, Ruddy thought.

Ruddy pulled on his clothes and then Mr. Gorilla. He was stiff and scratchy. He wondered if he should put on the gorilla head and gorilla feet. He tried on the head. He could not only breathe comfortably, but his breath was nice and warm and heated the air inside the suit.

He decided the big gorilla feet wouldn't feel good. He struggled to bend over in the stiff, scratchy suit and put on his boots. His boots felt awkward; it was difficult to see through gorilla eye slits. But he was getting warmer.

In the living room, Grandmother Silk gave a little shriek when a hairy gorilla lumbered across the rugs and polished floor.

She gave a nervous laugh. "Rudford! What a fright you gave me." Then her face calmed. "Your boots are on the wrong feet."

"Raughhghhh!" shrieked Mr. Gorilla.

"Rudford, this is serious. I can't get the garage door opener to work."

"Joe Penny will know what to do," boomed Ruddy through the gorilla face. He took off the gorilla head. It was deafening inside Mr. Gorilla. He struggled to change his boots to the right feet.

"Excellent idea. Where is he, anyway?" Grandmother Silk picked up the phone to call Joe Penny. "He will fix the garage door and bring the car around. Then we'll go out for breakfast."

But the phone was dead. His grandmother stood up, frowning.

"I wonder what the roads are like. Lucy probably can't get through, either."

Ruddy followed his grandmother into the kitchen. She lit the gas range with a match.

"Keep that hairy suit away from the flames." She reached down the gorilla neck and plucked up the tag. "It's fire-resistant, but let's be on the safe side."

Grandmother Silk turned back to the range and rubbed her hands quickly above the flame.

"I can heat some soup for breakfast," she said. "That's better than cold cereal." She had a terrible time opening the can since the electric can opener wasn't working. She had to use an old-fashioned kind. They had tomato soup for breakfast, and they ate crackers when Grandmother Silk finally found them in a cupboard next to the oven. It seemed to get colder in the kitchen.

The oven wasn't working.

The furnace wasn't working.

The refrigerator wasn't working.

Lucy's little television wasn't working.

Then they realized the worst thing.

The water wasn't running. Just a trickle of rusty water came out, then stopped. They couldn't take a hot bath. They couldn't run water for tea or hot chocolate. They couldn't wash their hands. They couldn't flush the toilets.

Now Ruddy was really stuck at Silver Lake alone with Grandmother Silk. His grandmother was looking stiff and sorrowful. Her lips were pressed thin.

"We can wash our hands at the zoo," said Ruddy to comfort her.

"Yes," said Grandmother Silk, "when

someone clears the road for Joe Penny to get through. When someone fixes the electricity so we can open the garage door for the car." She didn't sound reassuring.

The house got colder and colder.

Grandmother Silk got out another fur coat for Ruddy.

"It'll be softer than your gorilla suit." But Ruddy decided to wear them both, his grandmother's mink over Mr. Gorilla.

She managed to get a fire struggling in the fireplace, and they sat in front of it in Grandmother Silk's fur coats, Grandmother Silk and a hairy gorilla, until they got hungry again. For lunch they had more soup and some bread and butter. Ruddy just knew they would not get to the zoo.

He would not go to a party as a chest-beating gorilla. He felt miserable; he felt cold; he felt like a prisoner dragging around in his grandmother's fur coat.

For a little while, he looked out the front window, trying to determine where the driveway was under the deep white cover, and where the road lay beyond. He watched for someone to come plowing through the snow. But no one did.

It was the worst Halloween Ruddy could remember. His grandmother had forgotten all about missing the zoo party. But she had also forgotten to remind him to do his schoolwork.

Grandmother Silk took a cheesecake out of the freezer. "It's probably too cold in the house for it to defrost," she said. "We could have ice cream." But it was too cold to want ice cream. They took the cheesecake into the living room by the fire. The fire had gone out, and Grandmother Silk battled the wood and kindling to get it going again. She got soot on her soft hands and soot on her black suit and soot on the white sweater. Her fire didn't last.

They went to bed early after more soup and partially frozen cheesecake.

"Survival is exhausting," said Grandmother Silk.

Chapter Five

The next morning, Grandmother Silk came into Ruddy's bedroom. She was wearing a ski jacket over a white woolly bathrobe. She was wearing ski boots instead of high heels. Her designer hair was flat on one side.

"I'm going to see what I can do about

breakfast," she said. "It looks like Lucy can't get here again. Roads are closed. I sat in the car in the garage and heard it on the radio." She went downstairs.

Ruddy thought about soup again and decided he would stay in bed for the whole day. He curled up deep under the covers and dozed off in a little circle of warmth.

What woke him up was a terrific smell. Bacon! Lucy must have come. He jumped out of his circle of warmth and pulled his jeans and sweater over his pajamas. He decided against Mr. Scratchy, Hairy Gorilla but draped Grandmother Silk's mink over his shoulders.

Down in the kitchen it was warmer. But

Lucy wasn't there. His grandmother stood in her boots and ski jacket at the stove. She was turning bacon with a fork.

"There's oatmeal," she said. "I got water from the lake. Imagine that. Here we sat around suffering yesterday without water, and we're right beside all the water you could want. I just took a pail." She lifted out the bacon and poured off the grease. Then she put some bread in the skillet.

"We'll have fried bread with our oatmeal and bacon." Ruddy's mouth began to water. The bread sizzled in the skillet.

"After breakfast we'll get more water from the lake," said Grandmother Silk. "We'll flush out the toilets. We'll heat water and wash up." She sounded very happy. Maybe it was because of no high heels. His grandmother looked shorter. And softer.

The breakfast tasted as good as it had smelled.

After they had made two trips to the lake for water, they stayed in the kitchen till afternoon. It was warmer there with water boiling on all four gas burners. They had more tomato soup and grilled cheese sandwiches for lunch. It felt good to Ruddy to wash his hands and face.

"Someone will surely come today and fix the electric wires outside," said his grandmother.

But no one came. They sat in Grandmother Silk's fur coats at the table in the kitchen and read. Grandmother Silk was reading a very fat book about the Civil War. Ruddy had found *Freckles,* a book by an old-time writer, in his grandmother's library. It was so old, it had belonged to Grandmother Silk's mother. Freckles had only one arm, and even though he was a kid, he had a man's job. It was a good book once Ruddy got used to the old-timey language. The water on the stove boiled lower.

"I'm getting bored with the Civil War," said Grandmother Silk, slamming her book closed.

Ruddy was in an exciting part of *Freckles,* where Freckles had just caught the trail of poachers. "Get a better book," muttered Ruddy.

"What *will* we do?" cried Grandmother Silk.

Reluctantly Ruddy closed his book, marking his place with a blue-jay feather he'd found before the storm. His grandmother had made him rinse it with peroxide.

"Do you know any games?" he asked.

"Games?" repeated Grandmother Silk. She stared into her past, remembering. "Is chess a game?"

"Sure," said Ruddy, "but I don't know how to play it. Do you?"

"Ummm," she said.

Ruddy wasn't sure what that meant.

Grandmother Silk was quiet.

"Your grandpapa used to play chess," she said at last. "With his friends. On a little game table by the fire in the library. I used to watch."

Ruddy was surprised. Grandmother Silk never talked about Grandpapa. He had died a long time ago, before Ruddy was born. The only image Ruddy had of him was from the oil painting on the living room wall, just an old man with a lot of white hair and wrinkled hands. But he looked nice, and Ruddy wished he'd known him.

"I imagine we still have the chessboard around here someplace. Maybe I can remember enough of the moves to get us started. Goodness knows, I spent enough evenings watching!" She smiled at the memory, as if watching a chess game were one of the greatest things on earth.

She got out of her chair and Ruddy followed her into the library, where she rummaged around in the corner cupboard.

"Aha! Success!" She held up the square chessboard and a purple velvet bag that clacked with a hollow sound from the wooden chess pieces inside.

The library was cold, like the rest of the house, but Joe Penny had left paper and kindling in the fireplace. Grandmother Silk touched a long match to the paper under the logs, and the flames began to warm a little corner of the room.

Ruddy pulled the game table in front of

the fire and they sat down with the chess-board between them. Grandmother Silk separated the white pieces from the black and pushed half of them to Ruddy's side of the table.

"It's coming back to me," she said, look-ing pleased. "White Queen goes on a white square, and Black Queen goes on a black square, and the rest like this." As they posi-tioned the pieces, Grandmother Silk was *humming*. Like somebody younger. And happier. Maybe like when Grandpapa Silk was still around.

"Who are these two?" Ruddy pointed at the two tallest pieces.

"The kings. One dark, one light. Each person has his own king to start with. You

win, or *checkmate,* when you capture your opponent's king."

All the pieces were on the board now.

"Will you take the black or white?" Grandmother Silk asked.

"Black!" Ruddy decided.

Grandmother Silk smiled. "Then I start the game. White always moves first."

She studied the board for a moment. She chose one of the pawns, moved it one square forward, and the battle began.

As the morning wore on, Ruddy learned more about his grandpapa. For one thing, he was a patient man. He had to be. Chess took a long time to play. And he must have been very clever if he had won a lot. It wasn't an easy game. Grandmother Silk was clever, too. The pieces she had captured were piling up by her side of the board.

The fire in the fireplace was burning low when Grandmother Silk sat back and said, *"Checkmate!"*

Ruddy looked at his king. There was no way out. Grandmother Silk was grinning. He felt oddly pleased, even though he had lost.

"Let's invent lunch now," suggested Grandmother Silk.

"Then let's read," said Ruddy. He really did want to know what happened to Freckles.

Late in the afternoon, his grandmother said they had better stop reading and make another trip to the lake before it got too dark.

"I'm sure someone will come tomorrow," she told Ruddy. Outside, he could see a little slice of a moon in the sky, though it was not dark yet. They tramped through snow to the lake's edge and filled their pails. Ruddy had a big pail and Grandmother Silk carried two smaller ones. On their way back to the house, they stopped to rest and look at the curved slice of moon. Now Ruddy could see, ever so faintly, the rest of the moon, too.

"I haven't looked at the moon in a long time," said his grandmother.

Ruddy was glad he was there to look with her.

Chapter Six

They left the pails in the kitchen and then Ruddy showed his grandmother what he knew about laying a fire. He crumpled paper and stacked the kindling like a nest on top with air between. He settled the logs so they wouldn't topple over or smother the kindling.

"Air is as important as dry wood to a fire," Ruddy said.

"My," said Grandmother Silk, "aren't you a surprise?" She picked up the matches from the mantel and asked, "May I?"

"Okay," said Ruddy.

Grandmother Silk touched the flame to paper, and the fire began. She lit candles on all the tables. They sat in their fur coats in chairs pulled close to the fire. The flames leaped yellow and red and blue. It was a splendid fire. They leaned back and stared for a while.

Grandmother Silk said, "When I was little, my mother wouldn't let me get close to a fire. She was afraid I'd get burned."

Ruddy was so startled by the idea of his grandmother being a little girl that he almost didn't hear the rest of the story.

"One time," said his grandmother, "when no one was in the room, I moved very close. The fire was so pretty. I put my fingers on the grate."

"No," said Ruddy.

"Yes," said Grandmother Silk. "My mother heard me screaming and screaming. I was saying 'I'm sorry, I'm sorry' over and over. Blisters rose up on my fingers. I still remember the pain. I thought I was being punished for disobeying my mother."

"It was just the fire," said Ruddy.

"I know that now," said his grandmother.

"I'm very impressed that you are so intelligent about fires."

When there were only glowing embers and an occasional flit of a flame in the fireplace, Ruddy's grandmother closed the glass fireplace doors.

"I think there's a way to keep the fire going all night," she said, "but I, myself, don't know how."

Ruddy told himself that would be something to ask Joe Penny about. It would be a good thing to know. The house seemed even colder now, after the warmth of the fireplace. They blew out all the candles and Grandmother Silk beamed their way upstairs with the garage flashlight.

When Ruddy was in bed and half asleep, his grandmother covered him with something heavy. "It's your father's old Boy Scout sleeping bag."

Ruddy drifted off, warmer than he had felt all day.

Chapter Seven

No one came in the morning, so they boiled water, ate breakfast, and read in the kitchen. Grandmother Silk had pulled her hair into a ponytail. Her face was shiny, and Ruddy noticed for the first time that his grandmother's eyes were green.

By noon no one had come. Ruddy had

finished the *Freckles* book, and they found chicken noodle soup and fixed more grilled cheese sandwiches for lunch. Ruddy made a fire for later. There was nothing to do but homework.

At four o'clock, under a gray and darkening sky, they bundled up to go to the lake. Grandmother Silk put on a fur coat over her jacket. Ruddy pulled on Mr. Gorilla. He was glad that his grandmother didn't object to his wearing it outside. They took the pails and the big stew pot and the watering can.

Ruddy led the way. At the lake, they stopped.

"Before this snowstorm, I'd hauled water only once before," his grandmother said.

"Years ago your grandfather took me camping."

Ruddy tried not to look too surprised.

"Your grandpapa loved the outdoors. We used to take long walks together. Once when we courting, we made angels in the snow."

Ruddy stared at his grandmother. He tried to imagine a younger version of her in ski boots and jacket (minus the mink), making snow angels with Grandpapa. Out there in the shadowy, snowy light, he could almost see it.

"Can I?" he asked. "Make a snow angel?"

Grandmother Silk glanced at her watch, then at the nearly dark sky. She smiled. "You may."

Ruddy fell back and flapped his arms wildly. Snow flew into his mouth. It tasted like a snow cone—his only Halloween treat this year.

"I love to make snow angels!" he said.

"You make a lovely snow gorilla, Rudford," said Grandmother Silk. And Ruddy thought he heard her laugh.

At home, they hung the wet gorilla suit in the pantry. They ate by soft candlelight in the kitchen. Corned beef hash from a can, and eggs, good and hot and tasty.

It was after dark when they heard the rumble. Ruddy ran to the front window and spotted the headlights of a snowplow.

"Look!" he shouted to Grandmother Silk.

Soon after, a big giraffe-necked machine arrived. Ruddy saw the lights come up the long driveway. The machine stopped in front of the house. In the headlights, Ruddy could see men in hard hats cross to the side where the tree had gone down. One of them carried a flashlight, shining it up and down.

Grandmother Silk put on her fur coat again over her ski jacket over her white woolly bathrobe. She pushed at her hair.

"Good thing it's too dark to examine myself in a mirror," she said. Then she put on sunglasses even though it was dark out.

"Stay here, Rudford," she ordered as Ruddy ran to open the door.

He wanted to ask why, but there didn't seem to be room for a question in his grandmother's manner. Anyway, he didn't really want to be seen in his grandmother's fur coat.

Ruddy watched from the long windows by the front door. He could see Grandmother Silk cross in front of the headlights and then just a lump of shadow shapes.

When she came back in, she told him, "The electrical wires have been dislodged from the house and also from the electric pole. They said they can correct it in an hour or so. We are the last job on their list."

She looked out a window at the machine and the men in hard hats.

"They are not from this area. They have Kentucky accents."

His grandmother wrinkled her nose as if that were something bad. "They didn't even tip their hard hats," she added.

"Would that have made you like them better?" asked Ruddy.

Grandmother Silk gave Ruddy a surprised stare. Her green eyes kept up the stare but calmed in her face. Ruddy couldn't tell what she was thinking in her grandmother mind.

The Grandmother Silk from before the storm seemed to stiffen into her old self right in front of Ruddy. "We'll stay inside."

Ruddy found himself annoyed that the men with Kentucky accents had come to save them.

Chapter Eight

They watched from the window. The men from Kentucky were working on the side of the house. It got darker. Ruddy and his grandmother could no longer see the men except for the beam from the one flashlight.

"They've only got one flashlight." His grandmother sniffed. She found the big garage one. This time she did not tell Ruddy to stay indoors.

Outside they watched the men drive the big machine with the giraffe neck up to a high pole. On the end of the long neck was a box. One of the men got into the box, and it rose way up to the top of the pole. Two other men took the flashlight and went to work on the side of the house.

Grandmother Silk waved her flashlight beam to the top of the pole. The man in the box looked down and nodded a thank-you. He was pulling at wires. In his hand, he held some kind of tool. Leaning from the box, he fumbled and fussed with the wires.

Every few minutes the box would move sideways or a little higher. He must have control buttons inside the box, Ruddy thought. The man in the box never said a word, just fussed and leaned and held the wires to the post. The light beam from his grandmother's flashlight wavered. She sighed and held up her arm with her other hand.

"You can rest your arm on my head," Ruddy said, and he stood in front of his grandmother. She leaned against him and patted his head so softly that he wasn't even sure he felt it. He had to keep his neck very still. It seemed forever while, high up, the man in the box leaned and pulled and steadied the wires in the beam from their

flashlight. Ruddy's neck began to ache, but it made him feel more a part of the work being done. He stood a little straighter.

The two men finished working on the side of the house. They came to watch the man up in the box.

One of them sang softly, "Oh, she may not be real purty, but she sure can light my lights." A funny sound came from Ruddy's grandmother. Was it a giggle? Ruddy couldn't believe that.

All of a sudden, lights came on everywhere.

"Oh," cried his grandmother. "Oh! Civilization!"

After that, there was celebration in the air. Joe Penny came driving up in his truck.

And Lucy came. And they all sat around the table in the kitchen, drinking cocoa. Ruddy and Joe Penny, Grandmother Silk and the men from Kentucky. His grandmother had put on lipstick and changed to lighter sunglasses.

"We had three or four flashlights when we started—five o'clock this mornin'. . ." The Kentucky accent was softly blurred. "We must'a jus' kep' leaving 'em at folks' homes."

The hard hat guy who had sung about lighting his lights turned to Ruddy's grandmother.

"Much obliged for your help, ma'am."

Grandmother Silk smiled. "I am the grateful one." She seemed to have changed her mind about Kentucky accents.

Lucy took cinnamon rolls from the freezer and heated them in the oven. Grandmother Silk told her, "Sit down with us now, Lucy. I'm glad you're here, but sit down."

They ate hot cinnamon rolls with butter and drank more cocoa. They told stories. Lucy bubbled with gossip about how others had fared in the storm. It had been such an emergency that electrical workers had come from other states to help.

His grandmother's crisp talk mingled with soft Kentucky accents and Joe Penny's gentle voice.

Ruddy hoped Grandmother Silk would tell about being a little girl and burning her hand, and camping, and snow gorillas, but she didn't. She would probably forget how they had stared at the fire together. Grown-ups always seemed to forget stuff like that. Ruddy began to feel sad in the warm, lively kitchen amid the warm, lively talk.

Then Lucy said, "Why so quiet? How did you manage, being snowed in these awful days?"

Ruddy looked at all of their faces, and at his grandmother Silk.

"We stared at the fire," he told them. "We didn't have Halloween, but we learned chess. We carried water from the lake, and gazed at the moon." His grandmother turned softly in her chair. "Grandmother Silk cooked grilled cheese and bacon and

soup. I made a fire. We had a great time."

It was quiet for a long moment.

Then Grandmother Silk said, "Yes." She sounded slightly surprised. "Yes, we did, didn't we?" She took off her sunglasses. Her green eyes looked at Ruddy the same slow way she had looked at the bright slice of moon.

"My Ruddy," she said as she took his hand, "we did, indeed, have a great time."